ONE SHOE

One Shoe

Three Chilling Stories

S.R. Crawley

Words are Kisses Publishing

DEDICATION

I dedicate this book to my mom. Without her encouragement, I would not have had the confidence to keep writing. I also dedicate this to my children. Without them, I would have never accomplished my dream of becoming a published writer, I love you all!

CONTENTS

ONE

MICHELLE WINEHEART

Bernard, a typical married man, and father of two, was jolted fully awake when his wife yelled from downstairs, "Okay guys! Rise and shine, breakfast is ready!"

Must she be so loud? He groaned.

As he lay there staring up at the ceiling, he looked beyond the white sheetrock, wooden rafters, and shingled roof, into a nothingness only he could see. He heard bedroom doors open, yanking him back into reality. Both teenagers trampled down the stairs making loud thudding sounds.

I guess THEY are going to be just as loud as she is! he thought as he forced himself out of bed.

He sat up, stretched, and lumbered over to a chair where he had laid out fresh clothes the night before.

He pulled on his pants forcing in each of his legs before zipping and buttoning. He was even less graceful with his uniform shirt. Once he had put on his mismatched socks and his tired work boots, he headed to the bathroom.

Standing in front of the bathroom mirror, he mindlessly shaved. He heard his wife Eve, scream again, yelling, that his food was getting cold.

Silently cursing, he finished shaving and put the razor away. He wiped his face dry with a towel and noticed he had nicked himself. He stood there looking at it.

The bathroom light reflected the crimson color as it forced its way to the surface, then slowly trailed down his skin, tickling his face. The mirror image made him smile.

Bernard jumped when his wife again called for him from downstairs, this time more forcefully. "Bernard! It's getting late!"

He focused on the cut. He glared at the blood still on his face. Using his finger, he wiped the blood, put his finger in his mouth, and licked as if it were a lollipop. *It tastes like iron.*

He left the bathroom, grabbing his work jacket before going downstairs.

In a hurry, he said goodbye to his wife before getting into his work van and rushing to work.

The morning air was crisp, and the sun was bright. He rolled his window down to let the cool air blow through his hair. He believed the sensual pleasure of feeling the wind blowing through one's hair wasn't just for women. He thought it felt like delicate fingers running through his graying dark blonde hair.

He didn't mind when the first gray strands started to appear. He would pluck them out with a pair of tweezers. Recently the gray was coming in faster than he could pluck, and he didn't like it one little bit.

"Guess it's time to dye it," he said aloud to the aging face staring back at him in his rearview mirror. "It can't be too hard."

Bernard had been a natural when it came to electronics, including cable installation. He went to work for Delta fresh out of high school. The benefit of free cable for as long as he worked with the company was something he couldn't refuse.

Within five years, he was promoted to installation supervisor.

He had met Eve there. She had moved to Madison to accept the receptionist job with Delta.

On what proved to be a fateful morning, he was in the office turning in paperwork. When he came out of the main office, he saw her. She was standing behind the counter, helping a customer. She took his breath away.

She was not the model or movie star type, but the average, run-of-the-mill, girl next door type. But there was something about her.

She had long caramel-colored hair and the brightest

blue eyes he had ever seen. But what captured him most was her smile. It arrested the deepest part of his soul.

Bernard simply couldn't resist her, so he introduced himself. A mere six months later, they were married, and within the first five years, they had two children.

As the wind blew through his hair, he found himself thinking about their marriage.

They had been married for sixteen years and he was sure everyone believed they lived a happy, fulfilled life. Eve seemed content. She was always laughing with the kids. Everyone always seemed to have something to do or somewhere to go.

Eve and the kids often tried to include him in the activities, and he tried a few times, but he didn't enjoy the things they did. He invented excuses for why he couldn't go and eventually, they stopped asking.

Leaving his thoughts, Bernard entered through the pretentious security gates of the new Country Club Estates subdivision and took an immediate right onto Diamond Drive.

A large, genuine smile spread across his face. He saw her walking towards her new, jet-black, Miata convertible.

He had installed Michelle's Wineheart's cable and internet services earlier in the month and developed quite a crush on her. She had visited him many times in his dreams.

She saw his van, and she politely waved and smiled.

Bernard turned into her driveway and parked behind her car. He opened the dented door and stepped out. "Good morning, Michelle, isn't it a beautiful day?"

"Yes, it sure is. This is my favorite time of year," Michelle answered, switching her purse from her left arm to her right. "What brings you this way? Someone having a cable crisis this morning?"

Bernard gave a modest laugh, "I was on my way to do an installation when I saw you. I thought I would stop by and see if you were having any problems. We've had quite a few in this area this month."

Michelle smiled.

Was the smile just for him? Crossed Bernard's mind.

"How sweet of you, but no, not a single problem." She said.

He stepped close and handed her one of his business cards.

"If you have any problems, any at all, call me on my cell phone." A big toothy smile spread across his face.

He was close enough, her perfume hypnotized him. Not realizing what he was doing, he closed his eyes and breathed in deeply.

Michell's smile quickly faded, and she became concerned. *Did he actually just sniff me?* Her stomach churned and she started to feel uncomfortable.

"Well, thank you. If we have any problems, I will make sure my husband calls the company." She edged towards her car. "I'm sorry, but I really must be going,

I'm running very late," and she placed her hand on the car door handle.

His face reddened and beads of sweat broke out on his forehead. His fingers curled tightly and stretched back out as he regained his composure.

"Wait, before you go, let me give you a new receiver. There has been a defect in a few of them, and this might save you a service call." He smiled.

He walked to his van and opened the sliding door. He stepped inside, grabbed a brown box, and held it out toward her.

She moved closer to the door. When she reached for the box, he grabbed her wrist and yanked her into the van.

She had no time to react. She didn't even scream. Nothing but a quick gasp left her lips. Then everything went black.

Bernard was again behind the wheel of the van driving south on Highway 51. The remote highway had a long stretch of woods on both sides.

As he drove, he replayed the events in his mind. He wasn't sure what had happened. He didn't know what came over him. When he saw her eyes narrow, looking around as if she was hoping to see someone, he knew he had raised a red flag.

His heart crumbled and something else took over.

He glanced back and saw her tied up on the floor of the cargo van. He saw her eyes twitching behind strands of hair that hung in her face.

Slamming on the brakes, he made a sudden sharp left turn onto a gravel road.

Shoot! Just about missed it. He cursed to himself.

The abrupt turn rolled Michelle's bound body against the back of the passenger seat, making her moan.

He had stumbled upon this road by accident when he got lost, looking for an old rural farmhouse address to do an installation. The road was narrow, and he had been afraid he wouldn't be able to turn his van around. The winding of the road, if one could really call it a road, made the prospect of driving in reverse almost impossible. He was relieved when the road ended in a clearing giving him enough room to turn around.

Michelle was able to get the gag out of her mouth and she screamed.

Bernard hit the brakes and rushed to her, almost falling over the console between the seats.

He stuffed the cloth back into her mouth, and she gagged. He pulled it out, "If you promise not to scream, I'll leave it off."

His face was close enough to her she could feel his steamy breath. Her heart was beating hard enough she could feel the pulsing in her ears. She wanted to curl into a fetal position and wait for someone, anyone to save her. All she could do was gesture, promising not to scream.

He double-checked the cable he had tied around her hands and feet. Giving a hard tug, he was satisfied they were tight. He knew the cable wasn't the best choice for something like this, but hey, you make do with what you have.

"How about you sit up front with me? No one is going to see or hear you all the way out here." He grinned.

She tried to resist him as he pulled her out of the van, standing her on her feet. Before she could try to escape, he opened the passenger door, manhandling her with his strong arms.

She battled, but it was useless.

He picked her up and threw her into the passenger seat. He reached over her, grabbed the seat belt, and fastened it, whispering in her ear, "Safety first."

She pulled away from him, her eyes filled with terror and her body emitted a sound that even scared her.

He gave her a wink before slamming the door. He settled into his seat and put the van into gear.

Michelle shrunk into the seat, praying it would swallow her up whole.

She stared at him through tear-soaked eyes, thinking about how she had misjudged him, now she was paying the price. She had foolishly let her guard down. His two big meaty hands gripped the steering wheel and she saw him smile as if enjoying the proudest moment of his life.

Feeling the heat of her stare, he turned, not bothering to hide his smile, and stroked her tender skin.

"Well, if looks could kill." His smile turned into a hearty laugh.

The isolated road came to an end at the small turnaround. They were surrounded by thick brush and trees.

She could see ruts; proof humans did inhabit the area from time to time. Empty beer bottles and trash was thrown about.

He methodically placed the van in park and turned off the ignition. He left the keys, feeling confident he didn't have anything to worry about. He got out of the van and started around to the passenger side.

Michelle started screaming, pushing herself as far away from the door as possible.

He stopped in front of the van and slammed his big hands on the hood. She went silent.

He stared at her through the glass, as if he was peering into her soul. The sunlight flooded through the windshield, lighting up her face. He saw tears streaming, glistening. He heard the muffled sounds of her trying not to scream. Black shadows formed under her eyes from her mascara, and her lipstick had smeared across her face. He leered at her, as if in a trance.

She seemed more beautiful than before. She was a work of art, created just for him and for his pleasure alone. A sudden rustling noise came from the bush to his right. He was jolted from his trance, and he frantically ran back to the driver's side of the van. In one swift move, he had opened the door and leaped into the seat ready for escape. His fingers were on the keys when a rabbit emerged from the bushes.

Releasing a sigh of relief, his eyes followed the rabbit as it disappeared back behind the bush. "Well, what excitement!" He said smiling.

She was paralyzed.

Getting out of the van again, he came around to her side.

She conjured up everything she had, and she started screaming again.

Throwing open the door, Bernard fist-punched her in the face. Michelle went limp.

Reaching in and unfastening her seat belt, grabbing her around the waist, he easily pulled her from the van.

She came to, her head spinning, but she was determined not to make it easy for him. She was going to fight!

Bernard won the struggle and tossed her over his shoulder. One gray sneaker fell from her tiny foot, landing in the passenger seat.

Carrying her to the edge of the clearing, he bent and let her slide from his shoulder to the ground with a hard thud.

She landed on her back, knocking the air from her lungs. She managed a pained filled groan. When her lungs filled again with the precious breath of life, she continued to scream.

Using her bound feet, she scooted her body away from him, only gaining a few inches.

"Whoa there, where do you think you're going?" He snapped. He was no longer Bernard, beloved husband, father, and successful employee. He had become a predator.

Straddling her body, he kneeled, placing a knee on each side of her. His hands went for the zipper on her jeans. Terrified, Michelle started thrashing wildly, twisting, turning, and bucking.

Bernard tried to hold her still, but she was a wild cat.

Somehow, she turned her body over. Laying on her stomach, she bucked like a raging bull.

He was astonished at how much strength the petite woman had.

He lost his balance, sliding to one side. He straightened, "Be still!" he shouted, striking her in the back of the head.

Michelle couldn't hear him over her own screams.

Bernard used his strong bearlike claws to push down on her neck. "Lay still, I said!" he said through clenched teeth. He added more pressure, muffling her cries in the dirt. Her neck snapped, the screaming stopped, and she went still.

Standing, he slowly turned her over. Her eyes were wide, frozen in terror. Dirt and grass stuck to her pretty face.

Looking around, he observed his surroundings, not knowing what to do next.

He pulled her lifeless body into the thick brush. He hoped her body would not be found until he had time to leave town. He figured it would only be a matter of time before the police questioned him. Someone could have seen him at her house earlier. *A good time to worry about that now, huh?*

He looked at her one last time, wishing it could have been different. Getting into his van, he made his way back to the highway.

When he saw the Highway 51 sign, his nerves started to settle, he was in the clear.

Exhaling a sigh of relief, he reached to turn on the radio and saw her gray sneaker.

"Well, that ain't good!" he said aloud as he unfastened his seat belt. He reached and grabbed the dainty shoe.

Confirming there were no vehicles in sight, he rolled down his window and nonchalantly threw the shoe out, letting it hit the blacktop.

Through the rearview, he watched as the shoe tumbled repeatedly until it finally came to rest in the road behind him. Satisfied, he breathed another sigh of relief.

Turning the radio to a classic rock station, he turned it up. When his eyes returned to the road, it was too late. He missed the curve, jumped the ditch, and collided with an oak tree.

Bernard was thrown through the windshield and landed on the hood, where he bled out.

The next day, a family traveling in a baby blue station wagon drove down Highway 51. Dad drove while Mom sat beside him, enjoying the scenery. Their oldest daughter quietly stared out of the back seat window while her siblings slept.

The girl saw a gray sneaker lying on the road. "Mom, have you ever thought about why you only see one shoe on a road, never a pair?" She asked.

The mother giggled; her daughter always seemed to come up with the most off-the-wall things. "The thought never crossed my mind." The mother answered.

Hmmm, I sure have, the girl thought as she continued to watch out the window.

TWO

EUGENE YOUNG

Estell was a waitress at a local restaurant. Nothing fancy but they served good food and ice-cold beer, bringing in regular customers along with good tips.

She had one son named Eugene. Despite being tired and her feet hurting, she was in a good mood, because she was planning to celebrate his fifteenth birthday when he got home.

She left work early to pick up the shoes she bought him for his birthday. She wanted to bake a cake before he got home from school.

This was a special gift, so she had it wrapped at the store. She couldn't help but smile as the clerk carefully folded and taped the red and black checkered paper.

"You made a wise choice with these," the woman remarked, noticing Estell's excitement. "They are going to love it." She finished the package with a black bow and handed the gift to Estell.

Estell held the gift, admiring the beautiful wrapping. "He will love the shoes just as much as I will love the look on his face."

She left the store and waited with two others for the bus. The bus pulled over, and when it came to a stop, the brakes made their usual swoosh sound. Single file, they climbed up onto the bus. She was last.

As she deposited her coins, she looked for an empty seat. There was none. She moved up the aisle to find a safe place to stand. The bus took off and lunged her forward.

She caught herself by grabbing the back of a seat. A young man rushed to help her. He placed his hand on her back to steady her. "Here ma'am, sit here. He gestured to the seat he had been sitting in.

It's nice to see a young man with manners, she thought as she sat down.

"Thank you, any other day, I might have argued with you, but not today."

"Well, I'm glad to hear," he laughed. "I have a feeling I wouldn't win an argument with you anyway."

"No, you probably wouldn't. Thank you for helping me. If it wasn't for you, I would have been laid out in the aisle or something." She joked.

"You're very welcome." He chuckled.

They rode in silence until her knight in shining armor pulled the cord, signaling he wanted off at the next stop. When the bus stopped, he nodded her goodbye and was gone.

Estell watched out the window. She didn't notice cars as they drove past, she didn't notice the people walking on sidewalks, or even the children playing. She was replaying the moments between when she found out about the shoes Eugene wanted, and the time she decided to buy them.

Four months before his birthday, he came running into the house, letting the screen door slam behind him. He was swinging around a magazine someone had given him at school.

"Mom, look! I want a pair of these." He held out the magazine so she could see it. "All the kids at school already have a pair. Since my birthday is coming up, they could be my birthday present. Please, Mom!"

She took the magazine. He had drawn a circle around the ones he wanted with a Sharpie marker. She had no idea what she was going to get him, and this would help her. He would get what he wanted, killing two birds with one stone, as they say.

In the picture was a pair of white sneakers decorated with a big silver check mark. Nike Air Vapormax, was written under the picture. "Were they afraid to show the price? How much are they?" She raised her eyebrows.

"I don't know. It couldn't be too much if all the kids had them. He crossed his arms, wondering why she was making it sound like a big deal. It was his birthday after all.

"We'll see. You'll know our answer when you open your present." She tried not to let on that she was teasing him, but she let the tiniest giggle escape her lips.

"Alright." He went along with her, then trotted off to his room.

The next day, she started making some phone calls. Only one store carried those shoes. Eagerly, she caught the bus, thinking how happy Eugene was going to be.

"$155 dollars! For a pair of shoes!" Her voice was a little too loud. She knew the whole store turned and looked at her, she wished she had a place to hide. She nearly fainted.

The months before Eugene's birthday, she worked every available shift so she would have enough to buy him those shoes, but $155! Like most mothers, she loved her son and wanted to make him happy.

Her husband Harold worked, but his hours at the factory had been drastically cut. Money was tight. There had been several arguments over the shoes.

"That's too much money, Estelle, to be spending on shoes." He yelled. "Money that could be best spent on things we need."

During the last argument, he had forbidden her to

buy the shoes. She clamped her mouth into a tight line, causing creases in her forehead to become more defined. She was as mad as a farmer with a coyote in the hen house. She did not want to say something she would regret, so she turned from him, leaving him standing in the kitchen alone. She went into the bedroom, closing the door behind her. She made the decision that she would buy him those shoes. Harold slept on the couch that night.

When she arrived home, she hid the gift so Eugene wouldn't see it before she was ready. Harold was not home, She figured he was able to work this morning Either way, she wanted him to stay away so Eugene could have a pleasant birthday.

While Estell was at home baking him a cake, Eugene was at school hating the day and dreading to go home.

He had only slept a couple of fitful hours. He knew his mother had been going in earlier, working late and he had overheard the arguments about money Mostly, he hated that today was his birthday, and hated asking her for those expensive shoes! In his defense, he asked for them before things went south but that was beside the point.

Estelle heard the front door open and then quickly shut. She held her breath, thinking it might be Harold.

"Mom!" Eugene yelled as he threw his backpack on the couch.

Estell had just finished carefully arranging fifteen candles on top of a chocolate cake covered with cream cheese icing. It was his favorite.

"Whew!" She relaxed, knowing it was not her husband.

"I'm in the kitchen."

He decided earlier that no matter how guilty he felt, he would not disappoint his mom. The first thing he saw when he came into the kitchen was his cake, covered with candles, and his precious mom standing there with the biggest smile.

"Happy birthday!" She shouted, crossing the room with outstretched arms. She swallowed him up in a tight bear hug. His arms went around her waist, and he felt every ounce of love his mom had for him. He hoped she felt all of his. For the first time that day, he smiled.

Estell pulled out a chair, "Here, birthday boy, sit down right here."

He did as he was told while she pulled a lighter out of her pocket and began lighting the candles. Once they were lit, she slid the cake in front of him.

"Now make a wish and blow them all out." She instructed.

Eugene briefly closed his eyes, drew a deep breath, and blew them out.

His mother clapped her hands and began to sing loudly. "Happy birthday to you, Happy birthday to you." He didn't bother to hide his big smile.

Estelle knew she was embarrassing him, but she continued to sing every word. When she finished, she cupped his face and planted a big, wet kiss on his cheek.

"Oh, Mom!" He pretended to be disgusted.

But she knew better. She laughed as she went to get a knife.

The two of them sat at the cozy table while they both enjoyed a generous piece of cake and a large glass of ice-cold milk.

Eugene started to think maybe his mom had done what his dad told her. He was actually relieved. Once they finished their cake and milk, his mom cleared the table and put the dishes in the sink.

"I'll be right back," she said and disappeared.

Returning a few moments later, she was holding a store-wrapped present.

The smile immediately left his face.

His mouth opened releasing a sharp gasp. "Mom, what did you do?"

She saw the concerned look on his face, "You can straighten up your face, right now," she said. "Don't you be worrying about grown-up stuff, there's plenty of time before you have to do all that."

He started to stand, but his mother placed her hand on his shoulder, gently stopping him. She put the package in front of him and kissed his cheek again.

"All right! Don't just sit there, open it!"

He saw the twinkle in her eyes and knew it had taken a lot for her to go against his father, but she had done it anyway. He could not ruin this for her. "It's almost too pretty to open." Tears threatened his eyes.

"Open it already!" She pretended to be annoyed and gave him a backhanded smack on the arm.

"Owww!" He laughed and covered the spot where she hit him. "Okay! Okay!" He snickered as he ripped off the paper. When he removed the lid, guilt poured in, as if a faucet had been left on, overrunning, drowning him. He never should have asked for the shoes, he knew they were costly.

Inside the box was the pair of Nike shoes he wanted. They were white with silver trim and a big silver check mark on the sides. He traced it with his finger before setting them down on the table.

He stood, wrapped his arms around her spongy waist, lifting her into the air, "Thank you, Mom. I love you so much," and kissed her cheek.

She returned his embrace, and they stayed like that a moment longer. She was the first to break the spell. "Put me down, you crazy nut!" She protested.

He gently put her down and in turn, she cradled his face and looked him straight in his eyes, "You're welcome son. You deserve them and so much more."

A tear formed in her eye and pulled a tissue from her pocket she wiped it away.

"Try them on, I'm working tonight, so I have to get back to work."

Hiding his disappointment, he sat down in the chair and tried on the shoes. They were a perfect fit.

Eugene danced as he washed the dishes. He could not believe how good they felt.

He was grinning from ear to ear when he heard the phone. He dried his hands, and answered, "Hello."

"Hey, man!" It was Mike, Eugene's best friend. "I got a new video game. You want to come over and play it?"

His mom would be at work for a few more hours and he had nothing else to do.

"I'm on my way," and he hung up the phone. Eugene knew he should finish the kitchen, but he knew he would eat another piece (or two) of cake when he got back. He put a cover over the cake and raced out the front door.

He walked down the sidewalk leading to Mike's house, watching where he stepped because he did not want to dirty his shoes.

He looked up to see three boys, each much bigger than him, walking toward him.

Everyone in the neighborhood knew these boys. They were the neighborhood bullies, James, Alex, and Logan.

Oh, great! Eugene said to himself when he recognized them. Without missing a step, he moved to the other side of the road. He had not had any trouble with the boys, and he hoped to avoid it now. He had made it to the middle of the street when suddenly someone jumped on his back, knocking him face down on the street.

The massive weight on Eugene's back kept him pinned down. The fall knocked the breath out of him, and the weight flattened his lungs causing little room to inhale much-needed air.

His vision blurred and the taste of blood filled his mouth. The side of his face stung like a jellyfish had attached itself to his face.

The boy continued sitting on Eugene's back. "Hey! Where ya' going?" He recognized the voice, it was James.

Eugene felt something like a ball ping hammer whack him on the side of his head. His ears started ringing. It was deafening, but he could hear their laughter. He heard them yelling something, but he couldn't understand what they were saying. He had to get up if he was to have a fighting chance.

He ignored the pain as he got his arms under him and pushed up as hard as he could.

James felt Eugene lifting him. He hooked his arms and legs around Eugene and tightened his hold. This time James found himself on his back with the full weight of Eugene crashing down on him.

"Get him! Don't just stand there!" James screamed to the other boys.

Alex and Logan scrambled, each grabbing a foot. Thinking they had Eugene, James unlocked his legs.

Eugene felt James unhook, giving him his chance. He kicked both feet. One foot landed in Logan's adolescent gonads. Like a dying cow, he moaned, cupped his family jewels, his knees buckled, and he puked. The other foot caught Alex in the stomach, forcing him backward, pulling one of Eugene's new shoes with him. Alex landed hard on his backside, sending the shoe over his head and it bounced, landing a few feet away.

Eugene's face became a lighted torch. Adrenaline coursed through his veins with impetuous force. He glared at the shoe and then snapped.

He turned to face James who had maneuvered himself into a sitting position. Eugene stepped forward and hovered over a wide-eyed James. His mouth gaped open as if he wanted to scream, but there was no sound.

Eugene tightly clenched his fists and started punching, connecting on alternating sides of James's face, thrashing his head from side to side.

The sound of sirens made him stop and look up. Alex and Logan stood there, faces frozen in pure horror, then ran off like scared rabbits.

James took the opening. He staggered to his feet, his head swimming. He pulled back, blasting Eugene in the mouth, sending him down again. He kicked Eugene repeatedly as the sirens drew closer. The kicking stopped, and James bent closer to Eugene. "This isn't over bud! I know your mom works late. It would be a shame if she didn't make it home one night." James gave a final kick, then staggered off.

Eugene forced himself to get up. Fighting against the pain, he followed James, careful not to be seen. Eugene turned the corner just in time to see James entering an alley. He quickened his pace, came up behind the boy, and whacked him across the ear, sending him to the ground.

James's ear buzzed as if a thousand hornets were inside, and a blazing poker was stuck to the side of his head.

James rolled over coming face to face with what was now a madman, and his blood ran cold.

Eugene didn't remember picking up the rock and using it to crush James's skull.

Later found walking the street, Eugene was covered with blood and wearing one shoe. He repeated only one sentence, "I have to find my shoe. I have to find my shoe."

While Eugene sat handcuffed at the police station, a family in a baby blue station wagon was returning to their motel room. The girl in the back seat saw a white Nike shoe lying on the road. Quickly she pointed and yelled, "See Mom, look, look! There is another shoe on the road!"

Her mother kept driving, smiling, shaking her head.

THREE

BILLY MCCALL

Billy was an average run-of-the-mill kind of guy. When he graduated, like most who lived in town, he went to work at the steel mill. He enjoyed repairing things and was hired on as a maintenance man.

He was one of the few guys his age who had his place. It wasn't anything fancy, but it was comfortable and suited him just fine.

He didn't keep much food. He would grab fast food on his way home. However, he made sure his refrigerator was stocked with ice-cold beer. After all, what more could a guy want in life?

It was Friday night and he and a couple of his buddies were going to throw back a few beers after work. When quitting time arrived, he had his tools wiped down and was storing them away when his buddies, Steve and Mark came up behind him.

"You're not done yet? We're going to leave you, man!" Steve joked.

Bill laughed, You're not going to leave anyone. You gotta have someone buy your beer when you run out of money, right?"

Steve lost his smile and punched Billy in the arm. "Don't be a wise guy."

"Come on guys, let's get out of here." Billy announced. He locked his toolbox and the three guys headed to the time clock.

Once in the parking lot, they separated, going to their trucks. Each removed heavy, dirty work boots and put on regular shoes. Workers who drove trucks would wedge their boots upside down between the truck cab and truck bed. They did this so their boots would be out of the way while staying dry on the inside.

Steve was the first to leave the parking lot, rocketing past Mark and Billy. "Eat my dust!" He yelled.

Mark and Billy quickly got into their trucks and sped off to catch Steve.

Billy and Steve were the first to reach Rack-Em Bar and Grill. Mark brought up the rear. They slid out of their trucks and headed towards the entrance.

"Mark was the last one here, so he has to buy the first round!" Steve said, pointing his finger at Mark.

"Shut up!" Mark shouted at Steve as they walked into the bar.

Rack-Em was not a five-star bar and grill, but it

wasn't a hole-in-the-wall dive. Neither of the guys could be considered regulars, but they had their fair share of food and beer here.

Mostly, they met at Billy's house, but this Friday night was special. They each received a special performance bonus and they wanted to celebrate.

Steve rushed over to claim the last table near the pool table. Steve and Billy sat down first, and Mark headed to the bar to buy the first round of drinks.

"Shoot you a game of pool, loser buys the next round." Steve said to Billy as he headed toward the pool table. He pulled a dollar bill out of his pocket.

Billy walked over and selected a cue-stick, "You're on! He chalked his stick, waiting for Steve to finish racking.

Mark returned with the beers. "Get ready to get whooped," he warned Steve. "You haven't seen Billy play." He turned his chair so he could watch the game, "This is going to be fun!"

Billy lined up the cue ball, pulled back his stick, and sent the cue ball fast and furiously into the other balls, sinking both the nine and fifteen balls on the break.

Steve stood there, eyes bulging and mouth wide open.

Mark all but fell in the floor, laughing, "I told you so, man!"

Steve closed his mouth and snorted, "It's okay, the game just started."

Billy pocketed two more balls, then scratched.

"Ha! That's what I'm talking about. Watch this!" He laughed, bowing his chest out like a peacock. He bent over and took his first shot, pocketing the one ball. "I got cha' now." He shot twice more and made those too. On his fourth shot, he tapped Billy's eleven ball and it dropped into the pocket. He cursed under his breath.

Billy took his shots, sinking one ball after another. He called his pocket, aims, and sinks the eight ball.

Steve threw his stick on the pool table, and gave the wall a flat handed slap, "I'm going to get the beers!" And he stomped off.

Billy and Mark waited until they were sure Steve would not hear them and started laughing.

"What was that?" Billy asked.

Mark shook his head, "You got me."

Steve returned carrying four beers. He handed each of the guys one, then plopped down with the remaining two. The guys looked at him puzzled.

"What? After a whooping like that, I deserve two!"

Later, they parted and went their separate ways.

Billy growled when he heard his cell phone ring. His clock showed 3:30 am. He let it ring, letting it go to voicemail. The caller did not leave a message but called back.

Billy grumbled as he rolled over and answered. "This better be important," he mumbled.

"What? Hello!" A voice snapped.

Billy jolted awake, recognizing the demanding voice. It was his manager, David.

"I'm sorry, I a... What's wrong? Billy stuttered.

"I need you here, like now. Machine twelve is down and we have a deadline, we need the order out TO-DAY!" David barked.

"I need to..." Billy started to answer, but David cut him off.

"No!" You get here now, Mr. Shore is here, and if you want to keep your job, you'll make it snappy!"

"Okay! Okay! I'm on my way." Billy ended the call.

He didn't get home until after midnight. He was so tired, he promised himself he would shower first thing in the morning and fell asleep with his clothes on.

He stumbled to the bathroom. He slipped on his shoes and rushed out the door.

He sped towards the mill, hoping a cop wouldn't pull him over. He almost missed his turn and ran over the curb. The jolt caused one of his boots to tumble onto the road. He did not notice.

He was speeding when he swerved into the parking lot, throws the truck into park, jumped out, and reached for his boots, but there was only one. He looked down in between the truck bed and the cab, but no boot. He franticly shuffled items inside the bed of his truck, but still no boot.

Billy hurried through the door, clocked in, and grabbed his toolbox. He made his way to machine twelve. Bryan and Thomas bombarded him as soon as they saw him coming.

"Billy! So glad you are here. They have been on our backs, threatening to fire everyone if this order doesn't go out today!" Thomas twisted his wedding ring while leaning on one foot and then the other.

"I got cha' covered boys." Billy hurried and opened his toolbox and started the task. Within minutes, he found the problem, but Thomas stopped him.

"Here comes David!" Thomas yelled.

Billy froze, not sure what to do. They had been preaching to high heaven about safety, and he didn't have his safety boots on. If he's caught, they could make an example out of him. He decided not to chance it.

"Ahh, there it is," he said as he stood. "Gotta grab another tool. I'll be right back." He scurried in the opposite direction, hoping the bosses would not see him and call him back. He made a slight turn and hid in between the stacks of pallets.

"Where is Billy?" David yelled. He should have been here by now!"

"He's here and already knows what's wrong. He went to get something and said he'll be right back." Thomas answered, still twisting his ring.

Billy stayed hidden in the pallets, silently willing David to leave so he could fix the machine and get out of there before the bosses see him.

Billy's telepathy thing seemed to work. He watched

David pull his phone out of his pocket and answer it. He couldn't hear what was being said over the loud machinery, but he watched David leave and let out a sigh of relief before stepping out from between the pallets.

Billy didn't see the forklift, and by the time the forklift operator saw Billy, it was too late. The operator turned sharply to avoid him, but the forks struck a stack of pallets and they fell like dominos.

Billy froze like a deer in headlights. He never saw it coming.

Bryan and Thomas heard a loud commotion. They rushed to see what had happened. They rounded the corner and saw the forklift operator, frantically swinging pallet after pallet, tossing them to the side, yelling in Spanish.

A crowd had formed. They all stood watching, not sure what had happened. Then the forklift operator found what he was searching for. "Call 9-1-1!" He yelled, this time in English.

Billy was pronounced dead at the scene. He was carefully loaded into the ambulance as his coworkers watched. No flashing lights, and no sirens were blaring as they left the parking lot.

Earl sat checking his phone in the passenger seat of the ambulance when he looked up in time to see Bob fly through another intersection before the light turned red. They saw a work boot lying on the road, then they heard it hit the undercarriage.

"Well, I hope no one needed that," Bob said.

A family in a baby blue station wagon, hit the road early that morning. The mom wanted to up the chances of getting a great spot on the beach for the day. The oldest girl sat up front while her younger sisters and brother sat in the back. She enjoyed riding up front because she could see a lot more. She counted the palm trees as they went by. She spotted the one boot.

To her, this would always be the world's greatest mystery. "You know what Mom? When I'm older, I'm going to write a book, and it's going to be about how a single shoe ended up on a road."

The mother had read every little story, every sweet poem the girl had written. She knew beyond a shadow of a doubt, that if she put her mind to it, she would do it. "With your splendid imagination, I know it will be a fine book, and I will enjoy reading every word."

The girl smiled at her mother, then turned back to the window, hoping to see another one shoe.

ABOUT THE AUTHOR

Sherri Croom aka S.R. Crawley is an award-winning master of words, weaving stories and poems that captivate and inspire. She completed her studies at Faith Bible Institute, where she deepened her trust and wisdom in God. She persists in learning the art of words and verses. She belongs to two esteemed groups of writers and poets who share her love for literature.

She lives in Arkansas, battling the fierce mosquitos with her loyal husband, three brave children, and six adorable grandchildren. She enjoys spending quality time with her family and exploring new worlds through books and journeys.

https://www.facebook.com/SRCrawleyauthor

ALSO BY S.R. CRAWLEY

In this soul-stirring collection, S.R. Crawley invites you into her world—a tapestry woven from life's raw threads. These poems, born from personal experiences, resonate with authenticity. With an overflow of powerful emotions, Crawley's words become a gentle breeze, carrying kisses from her mind to your soul. As you immerse yourself in her verses, you'll discover that you are not alone; your heart echoes the same whispers.

Rhett is thrilled to help his mom with the yard sale—until a little girl picks up his beloved teddy bear, Teddy. But there's more to this encounter than meets the eye. The little girl lost her own teddy bear in a devastating house fire. Rhett faces a dilemma: should he hold onto Teddy or extend compassion to someone in need?

In this heartwarming tale, your child will join Rhett on a journey of empathy and generosity. Through Christian principles, they'll discover the power of kindness and the joy of sharing. Plus, the book includes coloring pages for creative fun and a short Bible study where your child can reflect on the lessons learned.

Bible verses from the International Children's Bible version illuminate the path of compassion, making "Saturday Morning Yard Sale" a cherished keepsake for young hearts.

A prayer journal is a powerful tool for spiritual growth, self-awareness, and building a deeper connection with God. Start today, and let your written prayers become a testimony of His grace and guidance.

The marriage of Arnvel and Irene was seasoned by trials, and etched with scars, including the heartache of burying not one, but three of their beloved children at a young age.

Yet, when life dealt its cruelest hand, it was Alzheimer's that cast its shadow upon Irene. The once-vibrant woman, now lost in the labyrinth of her own mind, slipped away from Arnvel's grasp. The State of North Carolina tore apart the fabric of their love, forcing Irene into a nursing home.

But Arnvel was not one to yield. He embarked on a journey that defied reason. His determination knew no bounds as he fought to reclaim what was rightfully theirs, a shared lifetime.

They say love is the only force that can move mountains. And Arnvel was ready to move the world itself to bring Irene back where she belonged—with him.

In this poignant tale of devotion, loss, and unwavering commitment, One Way Ticket to Florida invites you to witness a love story that transcends time, memory, and the boundaries of the heart.

www.ingramcontent.com/pod-product-compliance
Lightning Source LLC
Chambersburg PA
CBHW061317140726
47998CB00006B/2437